W9-CUC-746

Randolph Caldecott's John Gilpin and Other Stories

Containing:

The Diverting History of John Gilpin
The House that Jack Built
The Frog He Would A-Wooing Go
The Milkmaid

Frederick Warne

Published by
Frederick Warne (Publishers) Ltd, London
Frederick Warne & Co Inc, New York

This edition © Frederick Warne (Publishers) Ltd 1977

LIBRARY OF CONGRESS CATALOG CARD NO 77-081562

ISBN 0 7232 2062 X

Printed in Great Britain by W S Cowell Ltd, Ipswich

THE DIVERTING HISTORY

OF

JOHN GILPIN

WRITTEN BY Wm. COWPER

WITH DRAWINGS BY R: CALDECOTT

Showing how he went farther than he intended,
and came safe home again

JOHN GILPIN was a citizen
   Of credit and renown,
A train-band captain eke was he,
   Of famous London town.

John Gilpin's spouse said to her dear,
   "Though wedded we have been
These twice ten tedious years, yet we
   No holiday have seen.

The Linendraper bold

"To-morrow is our wedding-day,
    And we will then repair
Unto the 'Bell' at Edmonton,
    All in a chaise and pair.

"My sister, and my sister's child,
    Myself, and children three,
Will fill the chaise; so you must ride
    On horseback after we."

He soon replied, "I do admire
    Of womankind but one,
And you are she, my dearest dear,
    Therefore it shall be done.

"I am a linendraper bold,
    As all the world doth know,
And my good friend the calender
    Will lend his horse to go."

Quoth Mrs. Gilpin, "That's well said;
    And for that wine is dear,
We will be furnished with our own,
    Which is both bright and clear."

John Gilpin kissed his loving wife;
    O'erjoyed was he to find,
That though on pleasure she was bent,
    She had a frugal mind.

The morning came, the chaise was
    But yet was not allowed [brought,
To drive up to the door, lest all
    Should say that she was proud.

So three doors off the chaise was stayed,
　　Where they did all get in;
Six precious souls, and all agog
　　To dash through thick and thin.

Smack went the whip, round went the
　　Were never folks so glad!　[wheels,
The stones did rattle underneath,
　　As if Cheapside were mad.

John Gilpin at his horse's side
　　Seized fast the flowing mane,
And up he got, in haste to ride,
　　But soon came down again;

For saddletree scarce reached had he,
　　His journey to begin,
When, turning round his head, he saw
　　Three customers come in.

·The 3 Customers

So down he came; for loss of time,
 Although it grieved him sore,
Yet loss of pence, full well he knew,
 Would trouble him much more.

'Twas long before the customers
 Were suited to their mind,
When Betty screaming came downstairs,
 "The wine is left behind!"

"Good lack!" quoth he, "yet bring
 My leathern belt likewise, [it me,
In which I bear my trusty sword
 When I do exercise."

Now Mistress Gilpin (careful soul!)
 Had two stone bottles found,
To hold the liquor that she loved,
 And keep it safe and sound.

Each bottle had a curling ear,
 Through which the belt he drew,
And hung a bottle on each side,
 To make his balance true.

Then over all, that he might be
 Equipped from top to toe,
His long red cloak, well brushed and
 He manfully did throw. [neat,

Now see him mounted once again
   Upon his nimble steed,
Full slowly pacing o'er the stones,
   With caution and good heed.

But finding soon a smoother road
   Beneath his well-shod feet,
The snorting beast began to trot,
   Which galled him in his seat.

"So, fair and softly!" John he cried,
   But John he cried in vain;
That trot became a gallop soon,
   In spite of curb and rein.

So stooping down, as needs he must
   Who cannot sit upright,
He grasped the mane with both his hands,
   And eke with all his might.

His horse, who never in that sort
   Had handled been before,
What thing upon his back had got,
   Did wonder more and more.

Away went Gilpin, neck or nought;
   Away went hat and wig;
He little dreamt, when he set out,
   Of running such a rig.

The wind did blow, the cloak did fly
    Like streamer long and gay,
Till, loop and button failing both,
    At last it flew away.

Then might all people well discern
    The bottles he had slung;
A bottle swinging at each side,
    As hath been said or sung.

The dogs did bark, the children screamed,
Up flew the windows all;
And every soul cried out, "Well done!"
As loud as he could bawl.

Away went Gilpin—who but he?
His fame soon spread around;
"He carries weight! he rides a race!
'Tis for a thousand pound!"

And still as fast as he drew near,
'Twas wonderful to view
How in a trice the turnpike-men
Their gates wide open threw.

And now, as he went bowing down
    His reeking head full low,
The bottles twain behind his back
    Were shattered at a blow.

Down ran the wine into the road,
    Most piteous to be seen,
Which made the horse's flanks to smoke,
    As they had basted been.

But still he seemed to carry weight.
    With leathern girdle braced;
For all might see the bottle-necks
    Still dangling at his waist.

Thus all through merry Islington
    These gambols he did play,
Until he came unto the Wash
    Of Edmonton so gay;

And there he threw the wash about
    On both sides of the way,
Just like unto a trundling mop,
    Or a wild goose at play.

At Edmonton his loving wife
    From the balcony spied
Her tender husband, wondering much
    To see how he did ride.

"Stop, stop, John Gilpin!—Here's the
    They all at once did cry;   [house!"
"The dinner waits, and we are tired;"
    Said Gilpin—"So am I!"

16

But yet his horse was not a whit
    Inclined to tarry there;
For why?—his owner had a house
    Full ten miles off, at Ware.

So like an arrow swift he flew,
    Shot by an archer strong;
So did he fly—which brings me to
    The middle of my song.

Away went Gilpin, out of breath,
    And sore against his will,
Till at his friend the calender's
    His horse at last stood still.

The calender, amazed to see
    His neighbour in such trim,
Laid down his pipe, flew to the gate,
    And thus accosted him:

"What news? what news? your tidings tell;
    Tell me you must and shall—
Say why bareheaded you are come,
    Or why you come at all?"

Now Gilpin had a pleasant wit,
    And loved a timely joke;
And thus unto the calender
    In merry guise he spoke:

"I came because your horse would
    And, if I well forebode, [come:
My hat and wig will soon be here,
    They are upon the road."

The calender, right glad to find
    His friend in merry pin,
Returned him not a single word,
    But to the house went in;

Whence straight he came with hat and
    A wig that flowed behind,   [wig,
A hat not much the worse for wear,
    Each comely in its kind.

He held them up, and in his turn
    Thus showed his ready wit:
"My head is twice as big as yours,
    They therefore needs must fit."

"But let me scrape the dirt away,
    That hangs upon your face;
And stop and eat, for well you may
    Be in a hungry case."

Said John, "It is my wedding-day,
    And all the world would stare
If wife should dine at Edmonton,
    And I should dine at Ware."

So turning to his horse, he said
    "I am in haste to dine;
'Twas for your pleasure you came here,
    You shall go back for mine."

Ah! luckless speech, and bootless boast!
    For which he paid full dear;
For while he spake, a braying ass
    Did sing most loud and clear;

Whereat his horse did snort, as he
Had heard a lion roar,
And galloped off with all his might,
As he had done before.

Away went Gilpin, and away
    Went Gilpin's hat and wig;
He lost them sooner than at first,
    For why?—they were too big.

Now Mistress Gilpin, when she saw
    Her husband posting down
Into the country far away,
    She pulled out half a-crown;

And thus unto the youth she said
    That drove them to the "Bell,"
"This shall be yours when you bring back
    My husband safe and well."

The youth did ride, and soon did meet
    John coming back amain;
Whom in a trice he tried to stop,
    By catching at his rein.

But not performing what he meant,
And gladly would have done,
The frighted steed he frighted more,
And made him faster run.

Away went Gilpin, and away
    Went postboy at his heels,
The postboy's horse right glad to miss
    The lumbering of the wheels.

Six gentlemen upon the road,
    Thus seeing Gilpin fly,
With postboy scampering in the rear,
    They raised the hue and cry.

"Stop thief! stop thief! a highwayman!"
    Not one of them was mute;

And all and each that passed that way
    Did join in the pursuit.

And now the turnpike-gates again
    Flew open in short space;
The toll-man thinking, as before,
    That Gilpin rode a race.

And so he did, and won it too,
    For he got first to town;
Nor stopped till where he had got up,
    He did again get down.

Now let us sing, Long live the King,
And Gilpin, long live he;
And when he next doth ride abroad,
May I be there to see.

THIS is the House that

Jack built.

This is the Malt,
That lay in the House that
Jack built.

This is the Rat,
That ate the Malt,
That lay in the House
  that Jack built.

This is the Cat,

That killed the Rat,

That ate the Malt,

That lay in the House that Jack built.

This is the Dog,
That worried the Cat,
That killed the Rat,
That ate the Malt,
That lay in the House that
        Jack built.

40

This is the Cow with the crumpled horn,

That tossed the Dog,

That worried the Cat,

That killed the Rat,

That ate the Malt,

That lay in the House that

        Jack built.

This is the Maiden all forlorn,
That milked the Cow with the crumpled horn,

That tossed the Dog,
That worried the Cat,
That killed the Rat,
That ate the Malt,
That lay in the House
that Jack built.

This is the Man all tattered and torn,
That kissed the Maiden all forlorn,
That milked the Cow with
the crumpled horn,
That tossed the Dog,
That worried the Cat,
That killed the Rat,
That ate the Malt,
That lay in the House
that Jack built.

This is the Priest, all shaven and shorn,

That married the Man all tattered and torn,

That kissed the Maiden all forlorn,

That milked the Cow with
the crumpled horn,

That tossed the Dog,

That worried the Cat,

That killed the Rat,

That ate the Malt,

That lay in the House
that Jack built.

This is the Cock that crowed in the morn,
That waked the Priest all shaven and shorn,
That married the Man all tattered and torn,
That kissed the Maiden all forlorn,
That milked the Cow with
    the crumpled horn,
That tossed the Dog,
That worried the Cat,
That killed the Rat,
That ate the Malt,
That lay in the House that
    Jack built.

This is the Farmer who sowed the corn,
That fed the Cock that crowed in the morn,
That waked the Priest all shaven and shorn,
That married the Man all tattered and torn,
That kissed the Maiden all forlorn,
That milked the Cow with the crumpled horn,
That tossed the Dog,
That worried the Cat,
That killed the Rat,
That ate the Malt,
That lay in the House
    that Jack built.

A FROG HE
WOULD A-WOOING GO

A Frog he would a-wooing go,

                  Heigho, says Rowley!

Whether his Mother would let him or no.

With a rowley-powley, gammon and spinach.
    Heigho, says ANTHONY ROWLEY!

So off he set with his opera-hat,
            Heigho, says ROWLEY!
And on his way he met with a Rat.

With a rowley-powley, gammon and spinach,
   Heigho, says Aɴᴛʜᴏɴʏ Rᴏᴡʟᴇʏ!

"Pray, Mr. Rᴀᴛ, will you go with me,"
   Heigho, says Rᴏᴡʟᴇʏ!
"Pretty Miss Mᴏᴜѕᴇʏ for to see?"

With a rowley-powley, gammon and spinach,
Heigho, says ANTHONY ROWLEY!

Now they soon arrived at Mousey's Hall,

      Heigho, says ROWLEY!

And gave a loud knock, and gave a loud call.

With a rowley-powley, gammon and spinach,

      Heigho, says ANTHONY ROWLEY!

"Pray, Miss MOUSEY, are you within?"

Heigho, says ROWLEY!

"Oh, yes, kind Sirs, I'm sitting to spin."

With a rowley-powley, gammon and spinach,

Heigho, says ANTHONY ROWLEY!

"Pray, Miss Mouse, will you give us some beer?"

Heigho, says ROWLEY!

"For Froggy and I are fond of
good cheer."

With a rowley-powley, gammon and spinach,

Heigho, says Anthony Rowley!

"Pray, Mr. Frog, will you give us a song?"
    Heigho, says ROWLEY!
"But let it be something that's not very long."
    With a rowley-powley, gammon and spinach,
    Heigho, says ANTHONY ROWLEY!

"Indeed, Miss MOUSE," replied Mr. FROG,

   Heigho, says ROWLEY!

"A cold has made me as hoarse as a Hog."

  With a rowley-powley, gammon and spinach,

   Heigho, says ANTHONY ROWLEY!

"Since you have caught cold," Miss MOUSEY said,

Heigho, says ROWLEY!

"I'll sing you a song that I have just made."

With a rowley-powley, gammon and spinach,

Heigho, says ANTHONY ROWLEY!

But while they were all thus a merry-making,

> *Heigho, says* ROWLEY!

A Cat and her Kittens came tumbling in.

> *With a rowley-powley, gammon and spinach,*

> *Heigho, says* ANTHONY ROWLEY!

The Cat she seized the Rat by the crown;
   Heigho, says ROWLEY!
The Kittens they pulled the little Mouse down.
   With a rowley-powley, gammon and spinach,
   Heigho, says ANTHONY ROWLEY!

This put Mr. FROG in a terrible fright;
   Heigho, says ROWLEY!
He took up his hat, and he wished them good night.
   With a rowley-powley, gammon and spinach,
   Heigho, says ANTHONY ROWLEY!

But as Froggy was crossing a silvery brook,

Heigho, says ROWLEY!

A lily-white Duck came and gobbled him up.

With a rowley-powley, gammon and spinach,

Heigho, says ANTHONY ROWLEY!

So there was an end of one, two, and three,
  Heigho, says Rowley!
The Rat, the Mouse, and the little Frog-gee!
  With a rowley-powley, gammon and spinach,
  Heigho, says Anthony Rowley!

"WHERE are you going, my Pretty Maid?"
"I'm going a-milking, Sir," she said.

"Shall I go with you, my Pretty Maid?"
"Oh yes, if you please, kind Sir," she said.

"What is your Father, my Pretty Maid?"

"My Father's a Farmer, Sir," she said.

"Shall I marry you, my Pretty Maid?"
"Oh thank you, kindly, Sir," she said.

"But what is your fortune, my pretty Maid?"

"My face is my fortune, Sir," she said.

"Then I can't marry you, my Pretty Maid!"
"Nobody asked you, Sir!" she said.

"Nobody asked you, Sir!" she said.